But the woodcutter loved Snow White,
so he left her at the door
of seven dwarves, who took her in
and loved her even more.

Snow White and the Enormous Turnip

For Aoife and Francis

First published in 2008
by Wayland

This paperback edition published in 2009

Wayland
338 Euston Road
London NW1 3BH

Wayland Australia
Level 17/207 Kent Street
Sydney, NSW 2000

Series Editor: Louise John
Editor: Katie Powell
Cover design: Paul Cherrill
Design: D.R.ink
Consultant: Shirley Bickler

A CIP catalogue record for this book is available from the British Library.

ISBN 9780750255202 (hbk)
ISBN 9780750255219 (pbk)

Printed in China

Wayland is a division of Hachette Children's Books,
an Hachette UK Company
www.hachettelivre.co.uk

Snow White and the Enormous Turnip

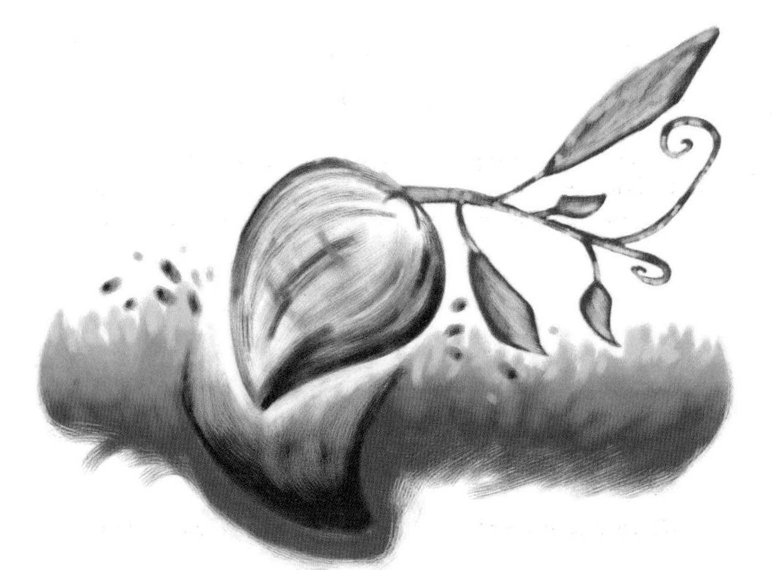

Written by Hilary Robinson
Illustrated by Simona Sanfilippo

WAYLAND

Snow White lived in a castle with
her stepmother, the queen,
who had a magic mirror and
was jealous, cruel and mean.

Each day the queen woke up and said,
"Mirror, mirror on the wall,
tell me I'm the prettiest
and the fairest maid of all."

The magic mirror flashed and said,

"Dear Queen, I tell you true,
Snow White is so much prettier
and far more fair than you."

The queen screamed out, "Woodcutter, take this cloak and big, brown hood.

Leave Snow White to die alone
in the heart of Turnip Wood."

Snow White planted seeds
and gardened every day.

One turnip grew so fat and round
that it stuck fast in the clay.

All the dwarves tugged and pulled.
Snow White's face turned quite pink.

"This turnip's just too big," she said.

"We need more help, I think."

At the castle, the jealous queen
asked her mirror on the wall,
"Am I now the fairest maid?"

"No. Snow White is fairer than you all."

The queen set out to kill Snow White
and thought of a wicked plan.

She dressed herself in a disguise
and down to the wood she ran.

The Seven Dwarves were with Snow White, as she rested by a tree.

“Try a tasty tart,” said the queen,
“It’ll give you energy.”

The queen was sure her plan had worked
'til a prince came riding round.

He knelt beside the pale Snow White
and kissed her lovely head.

And when she woke, he helped to pull the turnip from its bed!

Snow White got married to the prince.

The queen began to cry.

And, to celebrate, the dwarves served up an enormous turnip pie!

START READING is a series of highly enjoyable books for beginner readers. **The books have been carefully graded to match the Book Bands widely used in schools.** This enables readers to be sure they choose books that match their own reading ability.

Look out for the Band colour on the book in our Start Reading logo.

The Bands are:

Pink Band 1

Red Band 2

Yellow Band 3

Blue Band 4

Green Band 5

Orange Band 6

Turquoise Band 7

Purple Band 8

Gold Band 9

START READING books can be read independently or shared with an adult. They promote the enjoyment of reading through satisfying stories supported by fun illustrations.

Hilary Robinson loves jumbling up stories and seeing how they turn out. Her life is a jumbled up lot of fun, too! Hilary writes books for children and produces radio programmes for BBC Radio 2 and, because she loves doing both, she really does feel as if she is living happily ever after!

Simona Sanfilippo loves to draw and paint all kinds of animals and people. She enjoyed reading illustrated fairytales as a child, and hopes you will enjoy reading these fairytale jumbles, too!

But the apple tart was poisoned,
and Snow White fell to the ground.